SHORT ⦙
For cl

Oteng Montshiti

Short stories
For children
COPYRIGHT ©2020
CONTACT ADDRESS: OTENG MONTSHITI
P O BOX M1139
KANYE
BOTSWANA

E-MAIL ADDRESS: otengmontshiti@gmail.com
Contact number: (+267) 74 644 954

Table of contents

In the jungle-5
Wages of sin-13
Jimmy-31

Acknowledgments

Writing a book is a big task. Therefore I would like to thank our Lord Jesus Christ, my family, especially my lovely wife, who supported me.

IN THE JUNGLE

Long, long time ago in the deep jungle of Africa, there lived a young and energetic Lion known as the King of the jungle. The jungle was a magnificent place, with cascading flowers and waterfall, and rolling stones. The lion woke up every morning, roared and rattled the nearby hills. Then, he would pace across his kingdom majestically and take a cool bath under the waterfall. The water ran down his body and he would apply natural oil on his skin. Life was wonderful indeed.

As the time to hunt for a wife came along he refused to marry anybody. He felt women were too demanding.

"I am happy the way I am. I am enjoying my bachelorhood," he said in a thunderous and authoritative voice. Tortoise the wisest men in the land tried to give him some advice but he turned him down. The young lion enjoyed the life of partying and clubbing. He had nothing to worry about. That's to say, he had a leadership position, killed animals as he wished and had the most beautiful, oily skin in the whole world. He was the center of attention in the kingdom.

The years rolled by and his youthfulness diminished. He became old; his oily skin became dull and he had sunken eyes. His pace decreased. He would plod across the kingdom and couldn't take a bath.

Lion happened to be a friend of the most cunning creature in the kingdom, Mr. Fox. As the king became older and older, had no son, no wife, Fox took over as the King, but the animals were against that because Fox was very manipulative.

One day, he dashed into the cave where the Lion stayed due to old age and hunger was tearing him apart. He sat beside him on the rock, licked his lips and cracked a smile.

"What are you smiling at?" the lion asked impatiently.

"Your majesty, you can't go hungry like this. I have a perfect plan for you," Mr. Fox said throwing a cunning smile at him. He lowered his head and whispered something in his ears.

"I can't do that," he said angrily.
"Ok, if you play it that way you are going to die of hunger and starvation in this cave," Mr. Fox said brushing his head gently.

"Ok, ok, I want to live and I don't want to

die a painful death. Let's execute your plan," he said with eyes gleaming with excitement.

"Let's start now," Mr. Fox said as he leaped to his feet and stormed out of the cave.

He dashed into his house, grabbed a bell and broke the serenity of the kingdom. It was a custom that when the bell rang, it means something important had happened.Everybody dashed to the assembly area in the center of the jungle.

"Hey, you must watch where you are going. Elephant, why are you running blindly like that, you nearly stepped on me," An ant shrieked. "Sorry, run as fast as your little legs can carry you. Who knows, Maybe the king is dead, which means I will take over as the king of the jungle," Mr. Elephant said as he stumped the ground.

"You are a suspect, Mr. Elephant, how can you wish our king evil," he said as he joined the Elephant.

"Hey, you two what are you up to? You ruined my sweet sleep," snake smiled, the sound of the bell grabbed his attention and he slithered towards the assembly point. There was a huge stampede across the kingdom. In no time, the assembly point had swollen up with animals. Fox raised his hand to signal them to be silent. He strolled across the assembly point and descended to the podium.

"Ladies and gentlemen, welcome to this special meeting. I am going to be short and to the point, as you know, our king is old and is very sick. I have called you to tell you that you are more than welcome to visit him at the time of your choice at the Gog Caves," he said as he shed crocodile tears.

Everybody was touched because they loved their King very much. It was agreed that they would visit him on appointment basis only because a crowd might exaggerate his health condition. The following day, Antelope went to check up on the King but she never returned. Giraffe went there also but never returned. Everybody who went there never showed up again.

One day, Mr. Hare decided to check up on him, the mouth of the cave had plumes of thick dark smoke coming out of it. He interacted with Mr. Fox there. He glanced down on the ground and came to a halt.

"Good morning, Mr. Fox. How are you?" Mr. Hare greeted him revealing his spotless tooth.

"Good morning, Mr. Hare. Come in," Mr. Fox waved a hand at him with a flood of tears flowing down his cheeks.

"Wait a minute, not so fast, my brother, something looks funny here. I only see footprints of animals going inside but not going out," Mr. Hare gave him a quizzical look.

"Don't be ridiculous. There is an exit door at the back of the cave," Mr. Fox said cracking a cunning smile across his face. Hare refused to enter the cave, Mr. Fox ran out of patience and tried to grab him, Mr. Hare dodged and ran as fast as possible. He went throughout the kingdom and warned other animals.

Animals stopped checking up on him; the Lion grabbed Mr. Fox and ate him up. The king ultimately died of hunger and starvation in the cave and Mr. Elephant took over as the king of the jungle.

Wages of sin

"Hurray, hurray," a high pitched voice shattered the tranquility of the Sunday morning. The shouting interrupted Small Bear's thoughts, as the morning sun flooded his room.

"Who is that?" Small Bear asked himself. He rubbed his reddish, swollen eyes with the back of his paws.

He crawled out of his bed, strolled across the floor barefooted towards the wooden window, flung the curtains apart and glanced outside. He scanned the golden morning scene but he couldn't identify the source of the disturbance.

He rolled his eyes at the back of his head.

As he was about to turn away from the window, familiar figures emerged at the top of the cliff. It was Eagle's family, Papa Eagle, Mama Eagle and Grace the eaglet. They were deeply engaged in their morning training sessions.

Grace was riding on her mother's back, mounted high above the morning clouds, then Mama Eagle shifted beneath her, Grace tangled in mid-air and as he was about to crash on the sharp rocks below, her mother grabbed her. The session was repeated until Grace shrieked with joy in the air as confidence sat in. It was her final training session.

The clattering of the plates in the kitchen disrupted his thoughts; his mother was preparing English breakfast. He strolled towards the door, turned the handle, thrust the door open and zipped through the doorway. Down the stairs, he descended.

"Good morning, mum. Good morning grandfather," he said as he scrambled down on the brown wooden chair.

"Morning, son," they chorused.

"How was your night?" his mom asked from the kitchen hovering over the stove, boiling some tea.

"I slept very well," Small Bear answered, lifting his hands and clenching his chin.

"Tea will be ready in no time," Mrs. Bear shouted from the kitchen.

"Ok," Small Bear answered.

Small Bear threw a short glance at his grandfather; he was very old and fragile. He was the older version of his father, indeed. He had sworn in his heart he would never allow any death to happen in the kingdom. He would fight any evil doing and bring the perpetrators to book since the death of his father, (Remember his father was killed in their conflict with mankind in another book of mine entitled: Enough is Enough!!!)

In no time, breakfast was ready. Mrs. Bear strolled towards the dining table and placed a tray on the table with sugar, some milk and some scones. Small Bear poured some tea, scooped some sugar with a spoon, threw it into the hot water and stirred. He grabbed some scone, bites it, lifted his steaming cup of tea to his mouth and sipped.

When breakfast was over, Small Bear cleaned up the table while his mother cleaned up the kitchen.

Meanwhile, Mr. Hyena glanced up at the mountains and saw the Eagle's family deeply engaged in their training session.

"What a busy joy in their house," he said loudly to himself.

"Oh God looks at me, my father was killed in the battlefield decades ago and I am feeling lonely every day," streams of tears rolled down his cheeks. He mopped them with the back of his paw. He turned away from the window, paced across the floor toward his bed. Above his bed, swung side by side his photo and his father's. He came to a halt in front of them, thrust his hand and touched his father's image.

"I miss you, Dad," he murmured.

"I am going to retaliate one day. You fought for this kingdom and died in the line of duty. Today, people can't even remember your name. Everybody in this kingdom is going to pay deeply.

"Mr. Hyena decided to go out and while the time away at the foot of the mountain, cutting some firewood. He grabbed an axe in the shed at the back of the yard and strolled across the yard and paced towards the mountain. The sun was already towering over eastern horizons, warming his back as he cut some firewood. He straightened his back, sweat dripping down his face, he thrust his hand into his pocket, grabbed a handkerchief and mopped his forehead.

As the sun heightened and ascended along the vast body of the blue cloudless sky, tiredness sat in. He paced towards a nearby Mopane tree, crumbles to his knees and leaned against its trunk. He took a short nap which was disturbed by the cracking of dried leaves on the ground. Slowly, he pooped his eyes open and before him stood Grace the eaglet.

"Good afternoon, Mr. Hyena," she said with a golden smile across her face and a small lunch box tucked under her arm.

"Good afternoon, Grace. How are you? And what are you doing in the forest by yourself?" he asked as he mounted to his feet.

"I was at the top of the mountain and saw

you working down here and just thought that maybe you are hungry. Do you need some?" Grace the eaglet said as she stretched out her hands. Hyena moved closely, grabbed the lunch box and opened it.

"Wow, it smells nice," he said as he breathed in and out.

"Yes, my mother is a very good cook," she said rubbing her legs against each other.

"Come let's eat together," he grabbed her by her wings and crumbled to the ground. They feasted until they were satiated. Grace the eaglet leaped to her feet and glanced up at the rolling sun in the western sky. "Oh no! My mother will be mad at me. I must hurry home," she said as she gathered the lunch box.

"Not so fast, my friend. I would like to play hide and seek with you for ten minutes," he said pulling her down.

"The time isn't on my side," she pleaded .

"Just ten minutes, please," He said and his mouth curled into a smile.

"Ok, ten minutes," she agreed.

They paced across the thick forest, crawled up the mountain and settled at the top. They started playing hide and seek. Grace eaglet was standing at the edge of the cliff, Hyena pushed her off, screaming and dangling in the air, she landed on the rock at the foot of the mountain, crashed her little skull and died.

Nobody heard Grace's cry because everybody had gone deep into the forest to gather some wild fruits. As the night fell, Grace was nowhere to be found. Her parents searched for her all night long but all in vain. The next day, she was found dead at the foot of the mountain, due to severe head injuries. Her parents wept bitterly for their loss but nobody linked this gruesome murder to Mr. Hyena. To make matters worse, the overnight showers of rain had destroyed the evidence.

Few days later, as the sun rolled up in the eastern sky, Parrot the messenger brought heartbreaking news, another child was found dead, due to severe head injuries. When the news reached Lion's ears, he called a meeting at the assembly point in the center of the jungle.

"Ladies and gentlemen, I have gathered you today, to tell you that innocent children have been gruesomely murdered in my kingdom. The method of their death is the same and I think we have a serial killer in our midst. The perpetrator must be stopped and be punished severely," he spoke slowly with an authoritative voice.

"We must watch each other's back and report any incident that arouses suspicion. The perpetrator must be brought to justice," said Small Bear and everybody in the meeting nodded.

"If I meet him I will punch his face," said Hyena.

Everybody at the meeting was greatly

touched because nothing like that had happened in the history of the jungle. The wave of fear ripped through their spines. A killer was on the loose. The problem was that nobody knew whose child was next in his or her hit list. They threw short glances at each other.

"My child was brutally murdered a few days back. I have emptiness in my heart which can't be filled up," Mrs. Eagle sobbed. Her husband tapped her back gently to comfort her and mopped her tears with a handkerchief.

"It's going to be fine," Mr. Eagle consoled her. She leaned on his shoulder and sobbed.

"My child was brutally murdered too," Mrs. Giraffe shouted from the back of the crowd, everybody turned around and glanced at her. Everybody was crippled with shock and fear.

"Where is that person? I want to thank him because since these incidents took place my wife has been obedient. Remember, what seems to be a problem to others might be a blessing to another man," Mr. Hare pounded his chest with a fist as he giggled and the animals murmured in disbelief.

"I suspect you, Mr. Hare. You seem to be behind these gruesome deaths," Lion said.

"No, no, It was just a personal opinion and cracking some jokes," He said realizing the implication.

"Silence, Hare this isn't the time for your funny games we are talking about the loss of life," Lion pounded his podium with a fist and the animals leaped back.

Mr. Hare shut the hell up throughout the meeting. When the meeting was over it was nearly dark. Everybody was told to be on the outlook because nobody knew who was next in the predator's list. The night sailed through peacefully, the only disturbance was the whistling of wind overhead.

On the fourth day, the wind was howling overhead, lightning streaked across the dark sky and occasionally revealing the dark shadows or figures in the jungle, and thunder was rolling overhead. When the rumbling of thunder had resided, a shrieking sound tore through the night.

Small Bear was standing at the window, peering at the   dark clouds outside. Lighting streaked across the sky and revealed two figures at the top of the mountain. Another shrieking sound joined the rumbling of thunder overhead. Small Bear grabbed his raincoat and whistle; he dashed out of the house and ran through the rain. He ran as fast as his little legs could carry him. He zipped through the thick forest, plodded up the mountain and the noise eased when he reached the mountain top.

He halted for a moment, listen attentively but the night was silent except the whispering wind, roaring of thunder overhead and flashing of lightning across the sky. Then, he heard a humming sound in the nearby bush. As he approached it to investigate, he could hardly believe his eyes. Hyena was strangling an owlet.

"Hey! What do you think you are doing, stop it?" Small Bear yelled. Hyena turned his head over his shoulders, glanced at him. He was shocked.

"Small Bear, what are you doing here? I was just helping her out," Small Bear said pointing down at the owlet.

"No, he wanted to kill me. He told me that he killed Grace the eaglet and the child of Mama Giraffe," The owlet said with a shrilling and quivering voice.

"No, she is lying," Hyena said defensively.

"I believe her," Small Bear said. Hyena

leaped forward and pounded him with the rain of fists. He staggered; a stone tripped him and fell on his back. His vision was blurred. As Hyena leaned over him, Small Bear grabbed him by the neck, pulled him down, and rolled over and over on the ground with blood pouring out from the corner of Small Bear's mouth. They leaped to their feet; Small Bear's forehead burst open and blood spilling from his nose.

Hyena lurched forward and kicked him underneath. Small Bear twisted his face in pain with his hands between his legs; he ran out of breath and crumbled to a heap on the ground.

There was a siren behind Mr. Hyena and he came to a halt in amazement. He glanced over his shoulder; the owlet was blowing the whistle as much as she could. Obviously the whistle must have fallen down from Small Bear's pocket as they were rolling on the ground. Animals stormed out of their houses, ran through the storm, crawled up the mountain top. Hyena was arrested, tried and sentenced to death the following day. He was thrown into the cave at the edge of the jungle and the animals lived happily after.

Jimmy

A long, long time ago when animals could talk, there lived a tall, black and athletic young boy known as Jimmy. His mother died when he was very small. He lived with his father and stepmother, together with her children.

His stepmother hated him to the core. She didn't want him to go to school. Instead, she would send him to the fields to look after the cattle while her two daughters got the best education and attention at home. All these were done because his father was too traditional. He didn't acknowledge the importance of education. He thought that the best investment was looking after cattle, own your own one day and become a great farmer. After a few years, his father passed away and he was left under his stepmother's care.

He had a very handsome and powerful dog which went with him wherever he goes. They loved each other. They would talk together at the fields and the dog would warn him about any pending danger against his life. It would even tell him what was happening at home during his absence.

One day, the dog came to him licking his hands, and whispered in his ear, "Jimmy do you want to know your stepmother's top secret," it asked with a flash of a smile across its face.

"What, she doesn't have any secrets," Jimmy answered as he brushed its back.

"Ok, I was created by God to protect you and to make sure your purpose is fulfilled on earth," it continued licking his cheeks with its pink tongue and wagging its tail.

"What, to protect me how?" he asked. "Tonight, pray this prayer, "God reveal the secrets of my father's house," the dog paused; "you will tell me something strange tomorrow."

"I can't do that," Jimmy's face was white with fear.

"Be bold like a lion, I know you can. If you can't face your fear you can't face your destiny," it encouraged him. "Ok, I will, but promise me that God will protect me," he tapped his dog with his forefinger softly on the nose.

"The Lord is with you, don't worry, "it assured him as it brushed its head against his tattered trousers.

As the sun rolled behind the western skies and grayish shadows began to hug the earth, he headed his cattle home. Dinner was ready and a huge fire was prepared by his step mother. Stories were told and ultimately they retired to bed. Before Jimmy sunk into unconsciousness he said the following prayer, "God, reveal the secrets of my father's house" Then he fell asleep. As the time approached midnight, he was awakened by humming voices and footsteps outside the house. Then, a strange power paralyzed him.

He couldn't move or talk. The door was

flung open mysteriously, a dark shadow stepped inside and as it approached, he realized it's a baboon. His stepmother crawled out of her bed. She had long nails, burning eyes and wore black garments from toe to head. She scrambled to her feet, strolled across the room and stepped outside into the moonlight, where she met a strange group of people or witches to be precise.

Meanwhile, the baboon crawled under her blankets. Jimmy couldn't sleep, heart racing in his chest and suppressing his breath. Around half-past three in the morning the group returned. The door reopened and the baboon crawled out of the blanket and strolled out of the house. His stepmother crawled under the blankets and became a normal person again. Jimmy's heart was racing in his chest with fear.

"I feel like somebody is watching me, Jimmy," She yelled. Jimmy nearly leaped out of his skin, and then he sneezed.

"Mum, "he answered with a squeaking voice.

"What have you seen?" she demanded.

"Nothing, mum," he answered with a quivering voice.

"You are lying to me. I am going to hammer you if you don't tell the truth," she threatened him.

"Ok, mum, I saw you going outside that's all," he answered.

"Don't tell anybody what you saw otherwise I am going to make your life a living hell," She cleared her throat with a menacing voice.

"Ok, my mouth is sealed," he said as he moves his fingers along his mouth.

Then silence fell upon the room, cockerels broke the stillness of the dawn. The sunrays cut through the dark blanket of the night.

Since that time, Jimmy's stepmother hated him the more. She thought that as long as he was alive he was likely to reveal her top secret. She wanted him dead. She consulted a witch doctor who gave her muti that kills within a day. She went home and sprinkled the poisonous powder on Jimmy's food.

Meanwhile, the dog revealed everything to him in the fields. When he reached home, he took his plate, threw the food away without their knowledge and sat down as if nothing had happened. The day passed without any incident of a death.

The following day, she prepared a deep trench with sharp instruments like razor blades inside but in the middle of the night he grabbed his step-sister while she was asleep and placed her under his blankets. And the witches threw her into the trench and she died instantly.

The stillness of the morning was shattered by his stepmother when she discovered that she had killed her daughter. Jimmy pretended to be in sorrow while he was rejoicing in his heart. He kept on saying in his heart, "sweet revenge" and they buried her. Jimmy's stepmother was determined like never before and wanted to discover who was revealing her plans to him.

The following day, Jimmy went to look after the cattle as usual in the fields, his stepmother followed him without his knowledge. She hid behind a clump of bushes and watched him and his dog having a conversation. Then she realized that the dog had been revealing her evil plans to him. She quietly slid back home and asked a man with a gun to shoot the dog the following day.

Meanwhile, in the fields the dog revealed everything to him; "Tomorrow, I will be killed but be of good cheer because if I don't die you may never take full possession of your destiny.

It was written in the books of your life. You are a great man Jimmy," the dog said as tears welled up in its eyes.

"You can't die; I won't let anything bad happen to you. I can't live without you," Jimmy said with tears rolling down his cheeks.

"There is nothing that you can do about it. One last instruction, gather my bones and pray over them every day and at God's appointed time a miracle will happen that will push you into your destiny," he said rubbing its head against Jimmy's legs.

As the dog had foretold, it was killed the following day and its body was set on fire. Jimmy gathered its ashes, wrapped them in a plastic bag and buried them in the nearby hole as he was instructed by the dog while it was alive. It was a painful time indeed for him.

From that day, He went through hell on earth. He fetched some water from the river, cooked and even washed his stepsister's underwear. But he endured that pain. He thought of revenge but the last words of his dog gave him hope and encouragement.

One year later, the sun rose in the morning; the stillness of the day was shattered by the sound of a bell. As it was a custom, people rushed to the village square and when everybody had arrived and settled down, the King stood up from his golden throne and addressed his people,

"Good morning my beloved people," he greeted his people with an authoritative voice.

"Good morning your majesty," they chorused.

"Thank you so much. I will be short and straight to the point. My daughter has been sick lately and I have gathered the best medical practitioners to heal her but they have failed. I love my only daughter so much and I can't lose her," He said with tears rolling down his cheeks. One of his bodyguards' grabbed a soft tissue and gently wiped them away.

"If anybody heals my daughter, I'm going to give him or her half of my kingdom and marry her off to him if it is a man." He sat down; people started to split into groups and chatted. Jimmy was in their mist but he slipped away.

Everybody in the kingdom tried his or her luck but they all failed to heal the princess. As evening came the king furiously asked, "Is everybody here?" People looked around and noted that Jimmy wasn't there.

Meanwhile, Jimmy went to where he had buried his dog's ashes; guess what? he saw a red apple with a piece of paper attached to it written, "Let the princess eat this apple and she will be healed" he scooped it up and ran as fast as his little legs could carry him. When he reached there, his stepmother tried to stop him but he ignored her. He zipped his way through the crowd and stood before the king,

"Your majesty I will heal her and I am sorry for my late coming," he said as he bowed down before the king.

"Everybody has failed, what can a young, inexperienced person like you do? If you don't heal her I am going to cut your head off," Pounding his fists on the table before him and people leaped back.

He went to where the princess was and gave her the apple. She couldn't swallow it because she was very sick.

"Young man, I don't have time for mind games. If you don't heal her I am going to kill you," the king said with a stern face. Jimmy was very afraid because he knew that his word is final. He started to meditate upon the word of God and an idea struck his mind.

He remembered what his Dog used to tell him; "you must always ask God in faith and he'll give you the wisdom to overcome challenges". He crackled a smile, paced across towards the King's table and grabbed a knife. Then he sliced the apple and squeezed it between his fingers and an apple juice dropped into her mouth. The princess opened her eyes, and scrambled to her feet. She was healed instantly.

Everybody's jaw dropped. In the background, there was ululation and people gathered around him. His stepmother fell down and died of a heart attack. Jimmy approached the princess, grabbed her soft hand and kissed it. There was a huge celebration in the kingdom.

The king removed his crown from his head and placed it on his head. After, revealing everything to the king, he ordered his stepsister to be executed but Jimmy pleaded for her forgiveness.

"Your majesty, they meant it for evil but God in the secret courts in heaven meant it for my goodness. I will take care of her and all the glory goes to God," he flashed a smile across his face.

People were surprised by his mercifulness and followed his God. Even the witches repented and destroyed their idols and followed the ways of the Lord.

Jimmy stayed with the princess happily after.